Stolen Baby Amish

Hannah Schrock

Chapter One

Life was a blessing that everyone took for granted. Everyone was simply contented with the fact that they exist, without even realizing that their very existence, their very lives were gifts that no other human being could have given them. Only Gott had that power, that authority to bring whoever He wished into this world. He alone determined everyone's lives and fates, but sometimes people wished they had that very authority. For some, they wished they could create life as easily as Gott willed it.

Adam and Gabrielle Troyer were one such couple who wished they had such power. Married already for nearly seven years without a child to care for, they could not help but feel a little envious of all the new couples they saw during Sunday service who had already been blessed. Those new families' happiness only seemed to rub the depressing truth in Adam's and Gabrielle's faces: they couldn't have a child.

Gabrielle brushed the flour from her hands and sighed. She seemed to sigh a lot recently. It wasn't as though she were miserable; not really. She loved Adam the same today as she did when she married him. They adored each other. They both had fulfilling lives. He worked in his father's furniture store; a store that one day would become his. She had a part time position with an English tailors at town. They both had a great deal of friends within the Amish community as well as the English. Hardly an evening would go by where they weren't invited to dinner, helping out their siblings or engaging in a range of pursuits with various groups. But all of that couldn't hide the feeling that something was missing from their lives.

It didn't take a genius to work out what that missing thing was.

They were the only couple in the community without children.

Most people close to the couple understood that they shouldn't ask. Her mother had given up talking about it after seeing the floods of tears her daughter was reduced to whenever the subject was raised. They were trying. But Gott simply hadn't blessed them. Of course some of the older community members, who didn't really understand the situation, couldn't help but ask when they met. Gabrielle would smile and say in a little while and then rush home and cry her heart out for the rest of the day. The couple had even considered visiting an English specialist on the subject. Doctors could do marvelous things these days, Adam had said. He produced a newspaper article all about something called IVF and the countless number of childless couples it had helped. Gabrielle had read that article time after time. But despite her desire for a child she knew that she couldn't do that. Gott and Gott alone had the power to grant them the blessings of a child not a doctor. She put the article away and instead she vowed to pray harder. Gott would surely not forsake her.

She slipped the cookies into the oven and poured herself a large mug of kaffe. She sat down and began to read a few passages from the bible. Whenever she was in doubt or fearful she would read the bible and it would give her strength. At times she felt like Gott had abandoned her. But deep down she knew that that would never be the case; Gott never forgot his people. Today she felt doubt, and she was unsure of what to do. Amazingly, after seven years of disappointment, her normal courses were late. Three weeks late, almost four. Nausea had hit that morning. Adam was worried about her, but she dismissed it saying that Mrs. Jones in the tailors had spoken of a bug going around. She didn't know what to do? More than anything she prayed that she was right. She had none of the normal feelings that her courses were going to be appearing imminently. She wanted to share her hopes and suspensions with her husband. And yet she knew that he longed for a child more than her. Adam would have been more than prepared to visit that English specialist, going against their beliefs. She didn't wish to raise his hopes only to have them dashed if she were wrong. She was so lost in thought that she almost forgot about the cookies in the oven. She managed to catch them just in time. They would be a little crisp, but they would do.

A sharp rap on the door brought her back into the present. It was Naomi, her oldest friend, she was armed with a basket of a wonderful smelling kaffe cake. Gabrielle ushered her friend in and placed a large mug of kaffe in front of her.

"What is the matter Gabby?" Naomi asked, immediately sensing that something wasn't quite right with her friend. Gabrielle had that strange way about her that many other women had displayed in the past. It wasn't something that Naomi could describe. It was just there.

Gabrielle laughed nervously. "I'm glad you came today I have just gotta to tell someone." She started looking at the floor as though if she said the words then it simply wouldn't be true.

"You pregnant aren't you?" Naomi suddenly shouted with glee.

"Keep your voice down," Gabrielle scolded. Yet she couldn't keep the huge smile from her face.

"How long have you known?"

"I'm almost four weeks late and I had morning sickness for the first time today."

"What did Adam say?"

"He doesn't know yet."

Naomi looked at her friend with an inquisitive stare. "Why on earth not?"

"Because I'm not sure. If I told him and it turned out that I was wrong. Well, I'm not sure that he would be able to take it," she whispered.

Naomi shot to her feet. "Come on then," she demanded. "We can't sit around her all day guessing. Let's go and find out."

Three hours and a not insignificant examination fee later, Naomi and Gabrielle were heading back to the community. Naomi drove the buggy, taking care that the horse kept a steady pace, she didn't want to risk a crash. Not today of all days. Gabrielle had barely spoken a word since they had left the clinic. She just kept staring at the piece of paper in disbelief.

Later that evening Adam had come home from work. It had been a long day and Adam had a hard time dealing with a string of rude customers. The first thing he always enjoyed was a kaffe and cookie.

"How's the cookie?" Gabrielle asked.

"Good," nodded Adam, "A little on a crisp side maybe?"

Gabrielle grinned, "Yeah. Sorry about that. I was little distracted today."

"How's that?"

In a flash she pulled out the test results and presented them to Adam. He just stared in the same disbelief that she had in the buggy on the way home.

After seven years they were finally going to have a baby.

After the news sank in, both dropped to their knees and thanked Gott for his blessing.

Chapter Two

Little Noah had been nothing but the constant source of happiness in the Troyer Haus. He was not much trouble as some mothers complained their children to be. He had only brought more color to their already colorful home, always laughing and hardly ever crying unless he went hungry. Recently, Noah had just started learning how to walk by himself around the house. Sure, he still tripped now and then, but he seemed to be getting a hold of himself quite well. Still, he never failed to amuse Adam and Gabrielle who could not help but feel only happy whenever they were altogether inside their home.

That morning, Adam had gone to town for provisions so Gabrielle was all alone at home with Noah. She had been busy cooking up some lunch while Noah continued to practice his newfound walking skills. Chicken and creamy mashed potato were being lovingly prepared but more than once she had to stop her cooking to rescue her son who had managed to get himself into some form of difficulty.

"Hello," a deep voice shouted from outside on the porch. She recognized it immediately, it was her husband's best friend, Jared Schrock.

"Hey there, Gabrielle," Jared greeted as she opened the door. "Is he home?"

"Nee, he's down town. You'll be amazed at how much food we go through now we have Noah." Gabrielle explained. "Is it anything important? Or something I can help with?"

"Not really. I just wanted to talk to him about something."

"Let me guess, it has something to do with another failure at your attempt at a love life?"

"You make it sound a lot worse, the way you put it," Jared commented with a fake glare, "but ja, that's the reason I came over."

"I thought it would be. You haven't stopped by for a few weeks. There was bound to be another disaster on the cards pretty soon," Gabrielle retorted.

"Stop saying it like that. It sounds really degrading," Jared begged. "How do you even know about my failed love life anyway?"

"Adam talks about everything over meals," Gabrielle explained blatantly. "We keep no secrets from each other." She gave him a strange look that suggested that she knew a lot more about him than he could guess.

"I see," Jared felt slightly uncomfortable. "So how long do you think he'll be out?"

"He won't be long. In fact, he is a little later than I expected already. Would you like to come in and wait for him?" Gabrielle offered. "I know that matters of the heart should be talked through as soon as possible. There might even be a spot of lunch available."

"Denke," Jared replied as Gabrielle ushered him inside. Noah came running towards his mother screaming. He slipped next to her and tightly held on to her dress while poorly attempting to hide from Jared.

Jared knelt down, so he was on the same level, "And how is my best boy then?" Jared held his hand out for the little boy who reluctantly reached for it. Jared gathered him up in his arms and spun him around the air. The child squealed with glee as he turned. Both adults smiled in return as they all headed into the living room and sat down. Noah remained on Jared's knee and attempted to pull his nose.

"So what's it about this time?" Gabrielle smirked.

"Excuse me?"

"Listen, why not get a woman's perspective on the matter?" Gabrielle said. To be honest she wasn't sure why Jared's relationships ended in abject failure as much as they did. He was a handsome man and from her own knowledge of him he had a kind heart. And yet, she had lost count of the number of young women in the community he had been courting to one degree or the other.

"I don't know," Jared stammered. "I usually just talk to Adam about stuff like this."

"Come on, you can trust me on this," Gabrielle urged. "Besides from your track record Adam hasn't really been a great help has he?"

"Alright," Jared reluctantly replied. "So here goes…"

Just as Jared was about to relate whatever harrowing event it was that plagued him this time, they were startled by someone knocking heavily on the door. The knocking sounded urgent somehow. For some reason it scared Gabrielle, sending a chill down her spine. Jared immediately saw how anxious she seemed. "Hold on. Let me check out the window," Jared said as he got up to look out the window. He peeked through the curtains, evidently surprised at the person he saw standing outside.

Gabrielle saw Jared's eyes widen at whatever it was that he saw outside. For some reason fear grabbed her very soul, "Who is it, Jared?" she stuttered. Jared took a step back from the window as he turned to face her. He didn't speak. "Jared?" she asked once more, scared at whatever was out there.

"It's the police," he reported.

Having the police arrive at your home was almost unheard of in the community. A policeman coming to someone's home only ever signified bad news for the resident. They didn't come to spread joy.

"Do you want me to go answer the door, Gabrielle?" Jared asked.

Gabrielle slowly shook her head. "Nee, I'll go answer it. You wait in here with Noah," she replied as she stood up from the couch and headed to the door.

Heaving a sigh full of nerves, she opened the door to find both a policeman and a policewoman standing there. Their patrol car was parked right outside their house. There was little doubt they were in the right place. The policeman was the man closest to the door, and he appeared to be in charge. His expression seemed serious.

"Madam," the policeman greeted with a respectful nod of his head. "Are you the wife of Mr. Adam Troyer?"

"Ja, I am," Gabrielle replied, her hands starting to shake with nerves. "Good morning to you, Officer."

"Mrs. Troyer, I'm Officer Whitman," the policeman said. "I'm here on account of your husband."

"Ja, what's with my husband?" Gabrielle trembled. The policewoman behind Officer Whitman took a step forward as though she thought she might have to catch Gabrielle.

"Ma'am, I hate to be the one to relay this news, but your husband has been in a road traffic accident," Officer Whitman reported. "His buggy got hit by a car, about two hours ago."

Gabrielle did not know how to react. Her face froze in horror and she felt her mouth drop down out of shock. Her mind immediately flashed back to the moment before Adam left the house. It was just like all the other times. He made sure he had the list of goods that she had written. He had checked it twice and asked if she needed anything else. It had all seemed so mundane. So normal. But it was anything but. All he said was a simple, "See you later!"

"Is he dead?" she asked in a faint voice she did not recognize as her own.

The woman police officer stood in front of Office Whitman "No, honey. He's badly injured though. They took him to the hospital. We can take you there right now. I think that would be a good idea. You know, get you there as soon as possible."

Gabrielle nodded her head as she began to cry. How could this have happened? She could hear Jared approaching from behind, Noah still in his arms.

"Gabrielle what's wrong?" Jared asked looking at her and then at the police officers. Gabrielle found she couldn't speak and so Office Whitman related the situation in a very formal manner.

"Good morning, sir. I've just reported to Mrs. Troyer here that her husband has just been involved in a road traffic accident in town. He's been rushed to the hospital due to his critical condition."

Gabrielle watched Jared face turn from one of confusion into one of horror. She had no idea what was going through his mind, but she knew how much Adam meant to him. Those two had been childhood friends.

"I really am sorry about your husband miss," Officer Whitman stated as he slowly turned his attention towards Jared. "And how might you be related to the victim, sir?"

"I'm Jared Schrock, Officer," Jared replied "I'm not related. Not really. I'm Adam's best friend."

"And this little boy over here is your son, Mr. Schrock?" Officer Whitman asked as he started poking around with Noah who in turn playfully swatted away his hands.

"No. He's my son actually, officer," Gabrielle mentioned. "His name is Noah. He is very precious."

"Come on then, honey," said the female officer gently. "Let's get you to the hospital. Can you stay here and look after the boy, sir?"

"Well, yeah I guess," replied Jared unsure if he could actually look after a child for any length of time especially when he was going to be worrying about his friend.

"No," cut off Gabrielle, "Noah is coming with me to the hospital." She turned to Jared and spoke a little softer. "Jared can you come as well? I could use some support."

Jared nodded afraid of what they might find.

***

Jared never really liked hospitals. He had hardly ever spent any time in one, but every single visit to the hospital only reminded him of terrible things. Illness and death were at every turn. Nothing good ever came out of one. Now that they were here, he only expected the worst which only depressed him more.

"Hey, it's going to be alright," Jared assured her as they sat waiting for news. "I have faith in Gott that Adam will make it."

Gabrielle only shook her head out of doubt. "Ach, I don't know anymore. I'm scared, Jared," she cried.

"Honestly, I am too," Jared admitted. "But hey, don't let that get in the way. We just have to have faith in Gott and hope that he'll make it."

A doctor appeared out of a room and offered them a weak smile.

"Excuse me, are you the wife of Adam Troyer?" the doctor asked as she approached Gabrielle.

Gabrielle nodded. "Ja, that's me," she answered.

"Come through here a moment would you," she said guiding them into a private room. Once again she tried to smile and took a deep breath. "I'm so very sorry Mrs. Troyer. We did everything we could. The injuries were just too great."

Gabrielle lost the rest of what the doctor was saying. She screamed at the top of her voice. Hysteria set in. Not knowing what to do, Jared shoved Noah into the arms of the doctor as he embraced Gabrielle. The tears began falling for both of them.

"I'd like to see him," she finally said.

The doctor nodded.

"Give me a moment," she made to give Noah back to Jared. But Gabrielle snatched him first. Noah was all she had left of her husband. She was going to keep him safe. Very safe.

The pair sat in silence. Stunned. With Adam gone, Jarred felt like a huge part of his being had been taken away. But what must poor Gabrielle be feeling?

The doctor returned after a few moments and guided them through to another room. "We've taken a little time to clean him up slightly."

Gabrielle nodded a silent word of thanks as the doctor left them alone.

Adam lay in bed as though he were sleeping. There was no sign of the trauma that had killed him. Again, the tears started to well in both of their eyes. There was nothing they could do to stop them. Why would they want to?

Jared felt Noah pull on his pants and then watched as Noah turned his attention to the lifeless form of his father in bed. He pawed at him as though trying to wake him up. Gabrielle saw what her son was trying to do and slowly pulled him away from the bed before pulling him protectively to her chest.

"Nee Noah, you can't wake up your Daed anymore. He's gone," Gabrielle muttered to her son who had quieted down as she continued to cry. Jared instinctively put his arms around her to embrace her. She leaned in and cried even more as she repeatedly made the claim that her husband was now forever gone.

"Stop," Jared begged. He did not want to hear any more of the depressing truth. "We know he's gone. My best friend's gone. My brother's gone. Adam's gone. Things will never be the same again."

Chapter Three

The afternoon was bright. The breeze was cool. There were people taking their time roaming about. It was the weekend after all and the townsfolk seemed like they were going to enjoy themselves. There were groups of teenagers hanging around and families strolling about. Everyone looked to be having a good time. Gabrielle wanted to tell herself that she was just as happy as everyone else around her was, but she knew it would be a lie.

It had been seven months since Gabrielle had lost her husband to the accident. It turned out the driver of the car had been drunk. He had emerged unhurt, not even a scratch on him. Try as she might she simply could not forgive the man for what he had done; robbing her of her husband and her child of his father.

She had been trying to move on for the sake of Noah, but it wasn't so easy.

Adam had been a huge part of her life; her whole life until Noah came along. She didn't how to properly deal with her life now that he wasn't in it anymore. She was still able to go about her daily routines, but every day was always plagued with sadness. There were countless memories that she simply could not put aside. Raising Noah alone was tough. Although as was usual in situations like this, the community had come together to offer assistance. Bit by bit she was muddling through.

Gabrielle had come to town to run a few errands. She had always brought Noah around with her wherever she went. Her son, now twenty months, was her favorite company. She guessed it was because he reminded her of Adam. He was still her little bundle of joy ever since he came as such a miracle. He still never failed to amuse her with the faces he pulled. He was always so happy, that it was difficult to think of a day gone by when he had not made her laugh. The boy was her source of happiness, and she clung onto him more now that the love of her life had already passed on.

"Alright, do we have everything on the list?" Gabrielle asked herself as she fumbled around her shopping bags, looking through all her things to see if she had left out anything. She noticed that she still did not have the spool of thread that she needed to repair one of her dresses. Luckily for her, she had stopped right in front of an embroidery shop. It was quiet outside and the shop was only small. She decided to leave Noah outside in the stroller while she bought what she needed. She would only be a second.

"Noah, Mamm's just going to buy something in this store really quickly, ja?" Gabrielle told him with a smile. He grinned back in return. A woman charged past her and into the shop almost knocking her into the stroller in the process.

How rude Gabrielle thought. Why did people have to be in such a rush these days? What had happened to common curtesy?

She slipped into the shop waving gently to Noah as she did. It took her a matter of moments to find the color she required. She took the thread over to the counter.

"Just this please," she said passing the thread over.

"Sure thing," the man answered with a grin. "That'll be seventy cents, please."

Gabrielle could not help but smile as well. "Denke," she acknowledged and paid the man a dollar.

"You need anything else?" he asked, more in hope than anything. The shop was small and they needed all of the sales that they could get.

"I could go mad in a shop like this. But I had better not. Besides, I've got my boppli with me. So I had better get going. He'll be tired and getting grouchy in a minute."

"Yeah, I get you. I got kids of my own as well," the man replied. "So where's your kid?"

"He's back in that stroller over there," Gabrielle answered as she pointed at Noah's stroller through the store's window.

"There? I don't see anyone in it," the man said, leaning over to get a better view out the window.

"What?" Gabrielle asked. Fear suddenly overcame her, and she suddenly started anticipating the worst thing that could ever happen to her.

"I don't see any kid in that stroller, miss. It looks empty," the man stated.

Gabrielle flew out of the shop and peered into the stroller. As the man said, it was empty. She looked up and down the street, but it looked empty. Panic and fear gripped her body. She hadn't felt like this since that fateful day. The day that Gott had taken her husband away.

The shop keeper was right behind her. "Did you see anyone?" he asked looking just as worried as Gabrielle.

"No. There was no one," she screeched. "Noah! Noah!" Why did she leave him? Why? What a fool she had been.

"I'll go and ring 911 miss," the shop owner said heading for the door. "Don't worry, we'll find him."

Not knowing what to do, she started running up the street, "Noah!"

But the child was nowhere to be found.

Chapter Four

Jared had thrown himself into work since Adam's death. It was not the way he had wanted to spend his days, but without a wife to come home to nor a family to support, there was no other way to bide away his time. When he wasn't working he was trying his best to help Gabrielle and support her anyway he could.

Every Saturday afternoon he would take Noah on a long walk and allow Gabrielle a little time to relax and do some things that she needed to get done without a baby being around. He thought about the route he would take, down by the river. When Noah was older he would take him fishing. His heart sank. It shouldn't be him taking the child fishing it should be his father. But that could never happen now. So Jared was trying his best to fit in.

"Hey Jared, you're thinking about Gabrielle again, aren't you?" Reuben joked as he put down the last sacks of barley.

Jared scoffed. "Nee, I wasn't," he lied.

"Come on, I can see through your little lie. I know she's on your mind again," Reuben pressed.

Jared sighed and decided to give in. "Ja, so what if I was thinking about her again?" he fumed as he stretched his arms and back.

"Jared, I always catch you thinking about her. I'm starting to think that there's something going on," Reuben explained. Expressing what some in the community were already saying.

"Something's going on? Ach please!" Jared scoffed, "I was just wondering if she's fine and all. It's very hard for her you know."

"That's your excuse every time," Reuben remarked. "Don't you visit her home almost every day?"

"Ja, I do," Jared answered with a touch of anger. "I help her take care of Noah. Do odd jobs. What's wrong with that?"

"Nothing?" Reuben smirked. "Unless you think there is something wrong with it."

Jared merely brushed it off. "Nee, I'm helping. Since Adam's not around anymore," he replied with his face downcast. "Nothing wrong with that at all."

Reuben realized that he had just reopened one of Jared's emotional scars and immediately regretted it. "Ach sorry, I didn't realize," he apologized.

"It's okay. You don't have to apologize," Jared acknowledged. "It's just that I see how much she has had to adjust to life without Adam around. So I try to ease the adjustment process. That's all. I don't have anything better to do. I owe it to Adam."

"Are you ever planning to settle down, perhaps start a family of your own?"

"I don't know. I never really found the right woman for me. I've gotten together with so many women since the start of my rumspringa you know. All my past relationships are just failures, so I guess you can say that I've lost all hope in finding love."

"Don't lose hope now, my friend. You have still got a life ahead of you. I pray you'll find the one," Reuben said trying to make up for his earlier jests.

At that moment, both men turned to the sound of someone running up to the mill. It was Daniel who usually stood around with a clipboard as the two others mocked him for not doing anything physical. This time he was running, his feet clumsy as though he had never actually run before. He was carrying a little weight around the middle and the run was clearly not that easy for him. Whatever news Daniel may have brought for them was urgent indeed.

"You, Jared," Daniel called as he stopped right in front of them, struggling desperately to catch his breath.

"Wait, breathe first. Take a huge deep breath, Daniel," both men pleaded and Daniel took on their advice, catching his breath first.

"Alright, I'm fine now. Jared. You're needed." Daniel declared.

Jared looked confused. He had not done anything that could have gotten him in trouble. "What for?" he inquired.

"There was a phone call from the police station, they want you to come down the station as soon as you can," Daniel explained.

"Why would they want me?" Jared asked.

"The cops aren't the ones who need you there," Daniel clarified. "It's Gabrielle."

Jared's mind quickly flashed back to the last time the police and Gabrielle had been involved and he felt sick to his stomach.

"Why'd she call for me? Did something happen?" the words rushed out of Jared's mouth as worry consumed him.

"She won't say, though she did mention that it had something to do with her son Noah," Daniel reported.

Noah? Jared ran for his buggy.

Chapter Five

Jared had never actually been to a police station before. Sure, he knew where it was and even passed by it a number of times when he drove by in his buggy or walked around, but he had never once been inside one. It wasn't quite what he expected. He imagined a scene of chaos. Phones being passed from one to another, shouting, crime boards in place. But instead there was just a rather bored looking officer behind the desk.

"Can I help Sir?" he asked in manner that suggested he would rather do anything but.

"I got a phone call? From Gabrielle Troyer. Something about her son?" replied Jared.

"Ah! The missing Amish kid," the officer responded thoughtlessly. "You the father?"

A million thoughts flashed through Jared's head at once. Missing? Who was missing? Noah? The father? No. The father's dead. "Sir? Are you the father?"

"No," snapped Jared thinking that the officer shouldn't be so rude. "I'm just a close family friend. The father is dead I'm afraid."

The officer nodded like he had seen it all before. "Sit there," he pointed "I'll tell them you are here."

Jared didn't sit. He was too nervous. Instead he paced waiting for the officer to return. Instead another door opened and a female officer appeared, she smiled warmly. "Hi there. Are you Jared?"

Jared couldn't help but think that he had seen her somewhere before. Then it came to him. She was one of the officers that came to the haus to deliver the news of Adam's accident. "Yes, that's me. What's going on?"

She held out her hand and Jared shook it. "I'm Gemma. Gemma Wilson. I'm the family liaison officer here. I'm afraid that I have some bad news."

"You had bad news last time I saw you as well," he muttered out loud.

"Yes, unfortunately. Much of my time is spent being the bearer of ill tidings. Its young Noah I'm afraid. He's gone missing."

"Missing? As in lost?"

"Possibly. We aren't ruling anything out at this stage. But to be honest we are treating this as an abduction."

"What?" said Jared completely overwhelmed.

"You mean like a kidnapping?"

"Possibly. Again, things aren't clear at this stage. But we consider this more an abduction rather than a kidnapping. We aren't expecting a ransom demand. Mrs. Troyer isn't a wealthy woman. So we are treating it as an abduction."

"What's the difference?"

"An abduction is where the person is taking the child for reasons other than financial gain. There are a variety of reason why that might happen. I guess I don't need to spell some of them out."

"No," agreed Jared shaking his head and fearing terrible things.

"How did this happen?"

"Listen, you can get all the details in a moment. But Gabrielle really wants to see you. She is badly shaken. She considers it all her fault," Gemma continued. "Blame is no good in a situation like this. It just eats away at you. Try to convince her that it wasn't her fault. Okay?"

"Yes fine. Of course," agreed Jared. "Hang on. Why did I get called?"

Gemma shrugged her shoulders. "I don't know. You were simply the one she asked for. I sort of thought that you were her new partner."

Jared shook his head confused. "No. Nothing like that at all. Adam's only been dead a few months. I haven't even thought about…"

She raised her hand to cut him off, "My mistake sorry. No need to explain. Just me jumping to conclusions. I apologize."

That's the second person today who has implied that there was something between him and Gabrielle. The thought hadn't crossed his mind before. But now someone had put it there he found it hard to shift. But now wasn't the time. Poor Adam had only been gone a matter of months. And now this. The important thing at the moment was to provide support to Gabrielle and make sure that they got Noah back unharmed as soon as possible.

Gemma lead Jared through to a small office. Gabrielle was sitting, tears streaming down her face, in front of another police officer. As soon as she saw him she rushed into his arms. He held her close and felt a tingle through his body. He shook it off and concentrated on the matter at hand.

"What happened?" he asked softly.

"Oh Jared. It's all my fault. I left him for just a minute. I shouldn't have done. Noah. Where is my baby?"

"Hush," he said trying to sooth away the pain.

"I've betrayed Adam. What would he think? Noah took so long to come. He is so precious and now…"

Mention of betrayal of Adam immediately caused feelings of guilt to hit him in the stomach. If anyone was betraying Adam it was him with his feelings for Gabrielle.

"Come on now. You haven't done anything wrong. It is the person that took Noah that is to blame not you."

"Quite right," the other officer said. "I'm Captain Johnstone. I'm in charge of the case."

Jared nodded, "So what's been done? How close are you to getting Noah back."

The Captain sighed and immediately Jared knew that the police weren't close at all.

"We have officers searching the area, knocking on doors, asking folks. You know the sort of thing. We don't have anything clear to work on other than this rude woman."

"What woman is this?"

Gabrielle stopped crying for a moment. "A woman pushed past me when I went into the shop. She was the only person around. When I went in she must have come back out without me seeing and taken my precious boy." Tears started flowing again and Jared stroked her hair.

"We want to start a social media campaign. Get the message out there right now. The people of the town will come together. We have arranged a press conference as well. It would help if we had a photograph of Noah."

Jared shook his head, "Sorry Captain. We're Amish. We don't have photographs."

The Captain shook his head as though he were stupid for not thinking about it himself. "Of course. This is going to be a bit more difficult then. We will need a full description."

"Of course," spluttered Gabrielle. "I can tell you everything about my boy."

The Captain nodded, "Good. Miss I can promise you we will do everything in our power to get your boy back to you. These first twenty four hours are the most critical so we need to act quickly." Gabrielle nodded her head back in agreement and wiped the tears from her eyes. Jared looked at the Captain and prayed that he would succeed.

Chapter Six

Two hours later Gabrielle found herself sneaking out the back of the police station after telling Gemma she had to visit the bathroom.

She had just gone through a press conference where she sat and wept while Gemma put a comforting arm around her. Jared could only watch from behind the camera and wonder if it was against the Ordung. He decided he didn't care. If it got Noah back then it had to be worth it and no doubt the Bishop would understand.

Then she had spent half an hour with a police artist who tried to capture a likeness of the woman. The problem was that Gabrielle couldn't really remember anything significant about her. The more she thought about it the more frustrated she got. Then they moved on to a picture of Noah and this time she could recall every detail of his little face and his chubby hands. When the artist finished Gabrielle cried a bit more, the picture was so life like. She prayed this wasn't going to be the last image of her boy that her eyes would see.

Throughout the whole process she couldn't help but thinking the whole thing was futile. She should be out on the streets looking for her precious boy. Not wasting her time doing things for processes she didn't understand. Being Amish she didn't understand the power of social media and television. Not having these things she had no concept of how they could get the message out about the missing boy far quicker than hundreds of police knocking on doors. She simply thought that time was being wasted.

She had tried to whisper her concerns to Jared but he told her that the police knew what they were doing and she should try to calm down.

Calm down? She had thought. How could she ever calm down. Her boy; the only proof that her beloved Adam had ever walked the earth was gone. The precious boy that Gott had sent as a miracle had been stolen. She couldn't calm down and she couldn't just sit here. Every second felt like a lifetime. Each time the telephone rang she jumped hoping for news. She couldn't cope. She had to get out there on the streets.

It was amazingly easy to sneak out of a busy police station and she half wondered if criminals managed to succeed with such ease. She ran back to the shop where Noah was taken. It seemed a good place to start as anywhere.

"Miss? What are you doing here?" the shopkeeper said as she burst through the door, her face still streaked with tears and her hair sticking out from under her kapp.

"Adam would have been so proud of you," she said in a moment of clarity. She gently touched his hand and it sent a shiver through Jared's body. "Now, please. Find my baby."

He nodded and they both fell silent for a moment of personal prayer.

Gemma's window wound down again and she offered a gentle smile, "He's agreed. Can you get everyone from your community together in two hours?"

Jared smiled back. "If we hurry. And as long as you promise to take care of this one."

"Of course," Gemma shot back.

Jared gently helped Gabrielle to her feet. "Now promise me that you will stay at home and rest. You're going to need all of your energy."

Gabrielle nodded, "I'll do whatever you say. Just find him."

Chapter Seven

Gemma had wasted no time in getting the coffee pot on the stove when they returned to the Troyer haus. It was a good job because within fifteen minutes there were five Amish women in the parlor all offering soothing words of comfort to Gabrielle. Within half an hour, the place was crammed and Gemma had given up trying to remember names. The Amish women began some kind of vigil, praying for the safe return of young Noah. Gemma found solitude on the porch. As the sun began its descent in the sky, she found herself praying for the safe deliverance of the child.

She was fairly new here and had no previous experience of Amish people. This town had a very large Amish community and it had taken Gemma some time to understand their customs and though she still found their way of life baffling she had come to realize that people were essentially the same underneath the stuff of their lives.

Now take Gabrielle Troyer for instance. She was a pretty woman who would have had a great career in any field if she weren't Amish. But she had chosen a life devoid of any material goods, focusing on her family. These weren't choices Gemma understood but she could understand the heartbreak of losing a child.

Gemma's fingers trembled at the memory of her own lost child. How she had insisted on doing her duty, how a simple stint outside the public library had resulted in her falling a flight of stairs and losing the precious life within her.

"I brought you some kaffe and black current cake," a small stout woman with a kindly face came on the porch to give Gemma the food. "And I wanted to thank you for what you are doing for Gabrielle."

"I'm just doing my duty," Gemma smiled weakly. She took a grateful sip of kaffe.

These were hardworking people and though some people in the town viewed them as dim individuals sticking to ancient ways she could see the appeal in a life stripped of consumerism.

In the city she had come from if a child went missing no one but the family would get affected or bat an eye. But here, in this tight knit community it would hit every home. The devastation would be taken as a personal loss by everyone.

That was what one wanted from their community and the Amish had managed to preserve that in a world falling to pieces. That's what Gemma had wanted from her own circle of friends and family but had been sorely disappointed when they all blamed her for her situation, accused her of never wanting children. Gemma had to get away and she was glad her decision had brought her here, in a quiet community where people valued these relationships above all else.

Gemma thought of the missing child and how the chances of finding him were slim. She had seen it time and again during her six years on the police force. Children abducted were hardly found again, and when they were they weren't the same. She had seen families disintegrate at the loss of a child.

And unless the Amish community asked for help from the town the chances of finding Noah in the little window of time they had would be next to none.

Chapter Eight

The haus of Bishop Graber was small but cozy. His wife and daughters were at Gabrielle's haus with the rest of the women of the community. The men gathered in the tiny space feeling larger than they were because of the cramped space.

"It is unfortunate and we as a community will make every effort to retrieve little Noah," Aron Fisher said, "but we can not involve the Englischer community. Their ways are foreign and do not meet the Ordnung."

"It is Gott's will," old man Yoder said. "He gave Gabrielle the precious boppli to take the sting out of Adam's death and now Gott has willed that she must also mourn her boppli. She must accept Gott's will."

It was as Jared had feared. The community was averse to seeking any help from the Englischer town or to go

The Amish community took to the streets and the many paths in the woods and fields. They armed themselves with the picture sketched by the police artist and knocked on doors, stopped people on the street and interrupted people going about their shopping.

They spread word of the missing child and implored the Englischer town for kindness.

They haunted all the places children like. They visited the river and the clearing in the wood where a member a long time ago had made a host of treehouses so the Amish children might play. They kept a stringent look in the toy stores and children clothing store in the English mall to see if anyone bought clothes for a 20 month old boy.

And while the community was thus employed Jared sat with Officer Johnston and watched with wonder how the word of Noah's abduction spread like wild fire. Word of the abduction had gone as far as New York in a span of hours and people travelling on the highway near the town promised to keep a look out for any children of Noah's description in the other cars.

It was a miraculous invention and one that Jerad was sure made Gott's will greater, the spreading of His word more assured and a tool the Amish community should be using for the advancement of the Amish faith, not rejecting it as a work of the Devil.

"Now we wait and monitor the responses," Officer Johnston said leaning back in his chair a little. "If anyone finds anything they'll post it on our wall."

"But doesn't the lack of physical action make you feel helpless?" Jared asked who had been wondering at the restless feeling in the pit of his stomach. "How can you sit here and reply on the public to do your job for you?"

"There's very little the police can do in these situations other than wait for evidence to show up," Officer Johnston said irritably. "I need to put as many eyes out there as I can. What would you have me do? Run around like a headless chicken? What good would that action, just for the sake of it, do?"

"You are right," Jared sighed. "I'm sorry. I'm under a lot of strain."

"I can understand," Officer Johnston said. "Should I get you some coffee?"

"No, I think I'll go back and see if the community has found something," Jared said getting up to leave.

"How am I supposed to get in contact with you?" Officer Johnston asked. "If any thing happens."

"We have a communal telephone which is luckily in my neighbor's barn," Jared said. "I'll write down the number for you."

"I'll call you if anything turns up," Johnston promised. Jared thanked him then left.

The sun was low on the horizon, the bottom bleeding out as it sank slowly towards the other side of the world. When he was a boppli he had believed the sun died every day and Gott made it good as new every morning. It was Adam who had set him straight, telling him how the Earth turned and how the sun has been the same since our universe began.

Good Adam, kind Adam, companion on his childhood and youth. He had protected and guided Jared like a big brother and how had he treated Adam's memory? Jared now knew that he had very strong feelings for Gabrielle, that he saw himself with a wife and child and the wife had Gabrielle's face and the child was Noah. But he had failed in protecting Noah, Adam's son. Was Gott punishing him for wanting a gut woman like Gabrielle for his wife?

Jared met the people from his community on his way to the parking lot where they had all parked their buggys. None of them had seen hide or hair of Noah and it was with a heavy heart he headed back to Gabrielle's haus.

Chapter Ten

She didn't think she'd ever be able to laugh again. Whoever had abducted Noah had stolen her laughter as well. The physical need to hold her child was so overwhelming it took all of Gabrielle's strength of will to keep from tearing at her own skin and hair for grief.

When Jared had walked up her drive with that dejected look on his face she knew that they had lost the little window of opportunity that Gemma had talked about. It was crucial to make all the effort they could but the time was gone now and Noah hadn't been found.

Twice Naomi had to stop her from leaving the haus with just her cloak and boots. Gabrielle was convinced that only she could find her son, after all who knew Noah better than she? Gabrielle's restlessness had gotten so bad that Naomi had decided to spend the night with her.

They lay in bed together like they had used to when they were little girls, their hair braided in pigtails, their spindly legs nudging each other under the covers. It was different now. Gabrielle's face was drawn tight with heartache and Naomi's distorted with worry.

Poor Gabrielle, Naomi thought. She has always been unfortunate. First she had the loving husband but not the precious children. Then she lost the husband but attained the precious child. And when things finally seemed to be looking up with Jared courting her Gott saw fit to take her boppli from her. Maybe Gott deems only one form of happiness for her, not both.

"Gabby?" Naomi whispered in the silence, "Do you sometimes question Gott's plan for us?"

"Yes," Gabrielle whispered back. "I am not proud of it but sometimes I cannot understand why things happen the way they do and it makes me wonder if Gott is just and fair."

"I feel doubt as well," Naomi confided. "Do you think it is because of our doubt that Gott tests us more than others?"

"I believe so," Gabrielle stifled a sob. "But I wish that He had shown me the error of my ways without using Noah."

"Gott willing we will find him," Naomi held Gabrielle's hand. "Jared will not rest till he does."

"Jared is not Noah's father," Gabrielle said bitterly. "If Adam were still alive Noah would be safe in his bed. If Noah still had a father he'd be making an extra effort at finding him, he wouldn't be asleep in his own bed like Jared is at this very moment."

Naomi sat up in bed stunned. The community was sure there was a courtship between Gabrielle and Jared, a courtship everyone had approved of.

But Gabrielle's reaction right now negated that belief.

Naomi saw Gabrielle's tears streaked face in the moonlight and the flashing eyes and realized that Gabrielle wasn't angry with Jared, or think of him as any less for not finding Noah but she was angry with herself for allowing Noah to be taken.

"Oh, Gabby," Naomi held her sobbing friend.

"Where is my baby, Naomi?" Gabby cried. "Is he safe? Is he hungry? Is he cold? What if they have hurt him? How can I live with myself knowing someone hurt my baby and I didn't protect him?"

"Hush," Naomi soothed stroking Gabrielle's hair.

"Gott is punishing me," Gabrielle hiccupped, "He is punishing me for the sin of pride, the pride I took in Noah. He is punishing me for the sin neglect for when I sent Noah on walks with Jared so I might have an hour of peace and meditation. I have not thanked Gott enough for His precious gift f Noah, that is why he has been taken from me."

"You mustn't think like that," Naomi said gently. "We will find Noah. The community has reached out to the Englischer police and their net contraption. Jared said that people as far as New York have responded to the plea to find Noah. Someone will find him and return him to you."

"What if we don't?" Gabrielle whispered the one thought that haunted her every living moment since Noah had been taken. "I won't be able to survive that."

"Yes you will, Gabby," Naomi said tears streaming down her own cheeks. "You have survived much that any of us are capable of and Jared will help you survive this."

Jared. Gabrielle had focused all her frustration and anger at the person who had stolen Noah on Jared. Poor Jared who had been trying so hard to find Noah, who had been by her side from the very beginning not only now but since Adam's untimely loss. Good, kind Jared.

The thought of Jared didn't alleviate the pain of Noah's loss, it didn't make sleep any easier or the breath Gabrielle took any less hard to take but it reignited the flame of hope that had extinguished over the course of the day.

Chapter Eleven

The town is washed with the light of a new day, a stiff breeze whistles through the streets and hits Jared square in the chest. Jared closed his eyes against the sharp rays of sunlight. His head pounded a tattoo against his temples.

After a sleepless night Jared was in no mood to put in a full day at work but his nature and his upbringing wouldn't allow him to skimp on his duty. He walked on steadily, his head on fire and his heart in the pit of his stomach.

He had failed. He had convinced the community of investing in the Englischer social media and they had nothing to show for it. There was a lot of outpouring of love and support and many prayers across the globe but not a single sighting of Noah.

Jared smelled the enticing smell of kaffe in the air and spotted a small Englischer kaffe shop across the street. He normally wouldn't step inside such an establishment but he had forgotten to make his morning cup of kaffe in the morning and realized that was exactly what he needed for his headache.

His haus had felt lonelier this morning. There hadn't been anyone to make his kaffe or his breakfast since his mother had passed away. He usually had kaffe at Gabrielle's haus these days but he hadn't had the heart to face her today after he had disappointed her so thoroughly yesterday. A part of him vowed not to show his face to Gabrielle again till he had found Noah.

The bell tinkled overhead signaling his entrance in the Englischer kaffe shop. A young woman in a baseball kapp and green apron greeted him with a large smile. Jared ordered a black kaffe and paid for it. He stood to the side and waited for his kaffe and his eyes wandered to the people sitting in the kaffe shop enjoying breakfast.

There were young people taking pictures with their flat phones and old couples cutting their waffles and eggs in half and sharing their food in an age old ritual. There were families as well with young children chattering through their pancakes and blueberry muffins.

Jared felt pain twist his insides. The sight of the grinning children brought home what Gabrielle had lost. What he had lost as well.

A young child was playing amongst the tables with a bright red ball. The toddler was swaying slightly on his feet but toddling along after the ball, his giggles high pitched. Something about the child reminded Jared of Noah.

"Your coffee, sir," the girl behind the counter said.

The child turned his face around and Jared was convinced he was seeing things because the child looked so much like Noah it was unnerving. The child threw the ball up in the air with a joy filled whoop like Noah had done on many occasions while they had walked through the woods.

"Sir," the girl insisted. "Your coffee."

"What?" Jared said tearing his eyes away from the child with an effort. "Oh, yes, sorry." He reached out for the kaffe cup.

"Jalid!" the delighted squeal rent the air and short fat legs scurried across the floor. Jared watched, as if in a trance, the toddler rush towards him, trip and fall then pick himself up again the way Noah always did, his thin blonde eyebrows knitting in concentration. "Jaled!" he squealed again his tiny baby face split in a wide grin.

Jared scooped Noah up, his heart racing in his chest, his heart full of devastating love and his eyes brimming with tears of relief. Jared fell to his knees in gratitude to Gott for returning Noah, unharmed and happy.

Chapter Twelve

Gemma would always be grateful that she had been at Gabrielle's house when the dispatch had came through. Not having been able to sleep all night, Gemma had driven out to Gabrielle's house before going in to work to provide some moral support.

It had come as a shock when she had received the dispatch in Gabrielle's kitchen. Gabrielle, with her hollow eyes and flyaway hair, hadn't understood the significance of the message being broadcasted through Gemma's radio but when Gemma had told her she had leapt out of her chair and rushed out the house.

Gemma was now driving Gabrielle and her friend Naomi to the police station where Noah was being kept till his mother arrived to take him home safely.

"Where is he?" Gabrielle asked frantically as soon as she had entered the station. "Where's my precious Noah?"

"Right this way," Officer Johnston lead Gabrielle, Naomi and Gemma to a small coffee room where Jared was sitting on a sofa, Noah fast asleep in his lap.

"You found him," Gabrielle broke into fresh sobs. She came forward and took Noah from Jared, holding her child close to herself. She kissed his forehead, his cheeks, his eyes then she held him close again, all the while rocking back and forth.

"Mrs. Troyer," Officer Johnston cleared his throat awkwardly. "We're going to have to ask you to identify the woman responsible for the abduction. You'll be pressing charges of course."

"This isn't the time," Jared said standing in front of Gabrielle as if protecting him from the officer's crass demand.

"No wait," Gabrielle said rising up to stand beside Jared Noah in her arms. "I would like to meet the woman."

Officer Johnston led the group to the back of the station where a woman in her forties sat at a table. She had mouse colored hair that was thinning at the temples. She wore glasses and a perpetual moroseness about the mouth.

"Her names Candace Grape," Officer Johnston said. "She is registered as a mentally ill person and has been in psychiatric care for a few months., She was released recently."

"Why did she take Noah?" Gabrielle asked.

"Her psyche report revealed that she lost a baby," Officer Johnston said. "The baby was about your son's age. It broke her marriage and she recently had a manic episode when her ex-husband came to ask for their deceased infants clothes with his pregnant girlfriend."

Gabrielle clutched Noah closer to her. She could see her own sorrow in the downward curve of the woman's mouth, her own despair in the woman's sightless eyes. Her heart bled with sympathy for the woman who had stolen her child.

"I don't wish to press charges," Gabrielle heard herself say and she knew it was the right things to do. She had spent months hating the man who had caused the accident that had taken Adam from her and that anger and hate had consumed her, blinded her to the blessings Gott had given her. She wouldn't let that happen again.

"Are you sure?" Gemma asked astounded by Gabrielle's response.

"The Ordnung teaches non0violence," Gabrielle said calmly. "I will not persecute a woman who is already haunted by the loss of her child. Send her back to the institution where she was getting help and rehabilitate her to work with children. We should help her rather than punish her for her loss."

"I can't say I understand you," Officer Johnston said. "But I do respect your decision."
"I have my son back," Gabrielle kissed Noah's hair. "I do not need revenge on anyone as well."

Jared was proud of Gabrielle's decision and helped her through the remaining paper work to officially release Noah. After the long day when Noah finally woke up his eyes grew bright with delight at the sight of his mother's face. Gabrielle felt like her heart would rip out of her chest in happiness. She kissed her son's pink cheeks and allowed Jared to take them home.

After

"You shouldn't spoil him like that," Gabrielle insisted.

"Let me indulge a little," Jared chuckled. "A boy needs his toys."

"A bike is not a toy!" Gabrielle tried to be stern but the sheepish grin on Jared and Noah's faces made her relent. "Oh, alright. But he gets nothing for Christmas!"

"You have a deal," Jared said. Noah whooped for joy and climbed the red tricycle Jared had unloaded from his buggy.

They sat on the porch and drank kaffe and watched Noah boke around the yard. It was a companionable silence and their courtship had developed in this silence, forging a bond around the little boy in front of them and Adam who's presence they felt as a blessing of their eventual union.

Jared and Gabrielle had decided to marry a year from the day Noah had been found again in the Englischer town. Jared had expressed his wish to be a father to Noah and a husband to Gabrielle and to his relief she had expressed a desire to hear those words.

The community had been pleased by their decision and preparations for their union were under way.

"Do you remember?" Gabrielle said quietly, "The day Adam… you had come to discuss another courtship gone wrong?"

"How could I forget?" Jared smiled ruefully.

"Remember I said I could help you with your love life?"

"And I guess you did."

"Yes, but I'd never thought it would be so literal when I said it."

"Gott works in strange ways," Jared laughed.

"He does indeed," Gabrielle said sending a prayer of thanks up to Gott for blessing her with a complete family at last.

The End

Made in the USA
Middletown, DE
13 July 2023

35091934R00050